This book belongs to:

This book is dedicated to my parents, family and friends. To all the youth all over the world, remember that "Little People Can Do Big Things Too!" - Mikey

Special thanks to my Mom for teaching me that I can do all things. Phil 4:13

# Mikey Learns about Business

## Written by Mikey Wren

Illustrated by Donald L. Hill, MBA
Writing Coach/Creativity Specialist: Shamirrah Hill, M.A.

Printed in the United States of America
ISBN-13: 978-1545592632

One hot summer day, 9-year-old Mikey was leaving summer camp with his mom and little sister. On the way out, they passed a vending machine filled with chips, cookies and candy. "Mom, can I have one of the snacks in the vending machine?!" he asked. "No, not today," she said.

Mikey's mom looked at Mikey and asked, "Mikey, did you know that all the money you put into that machine goes to the owner of the machine? If you had your own machine, all the money would go to you." Mikey thought about this for a while, then said, "Mom, can I have a vending machine?" Mikey's mom giggled and said, "I don't think so, Mikey. Running a business is a lot of work. You're too young to own a business."

As they pulled into their driveway, Mikey's mom noticed jump ropes, balls, and race cars all over the front yard. "Mikey, go to the basement and grab a box to store all of your toys in," she said.

As Mikey headed down the basement steps, he said under his breath, "I will prove to them that I can own my own business." All of a sudden, a voice came from the back of the basement. "Hey!" Mikey responded, "Mom? Dad? Was that you?" The voice called out again. "Hey!" Mikey walked to the back of the basement. "Down here," said the voice. Mikey began to move things around until he saw a brown leather briefcase with two leather straps and two gold buckles on it. The briefcase began to speak again. "Hi Mikey." Mikey jumped back. "My name is Biz," the briefcase said. Mikey stared at Biz with a puzzled look on his face. Biz, the briefcase, spoke again. "You look sad, Mikey. What's wrong?"

"Well," Mikey explained, "my parents don't believe I can run a business. I want to prove to them that I can. The problem is, I don't know anything about starting a business." Biz smiled and said to Mikey, "Don't worry; I know everything about business! I'll be your mentor." "What's a mentor?" Mikey asked. Biz explained, "A mentor gives someone advice and shows them how to do things. You can ask me anything you need to know about business and I'll help you." "Really?! Can we get started right now?!" Mikey asked.

"Sure!" Biz said. Biz asked Mikey what type of business he wanted to start and why he wanted to own a business. "I want to own a vending machine business so I can eat all the snacks in the machine!" Mikey said. Biz smiled and explained that this was not a good reason to start a business. Mikey thought some more, then said, "Well, I also want to make lots of money, be a leader in my community, and help others." "Those are great reasons to own a business!" Biz said.

Biz told Mikey that the first thing he would need is a business plan. "What's a business plan?" Mikey asked. Biz explained, "It's a document that explains what you will sell and how your business will make money." Biz gave Mikey a sheet of paper. "You can write down your business plan ideas on this sheet of paper," Biz said. "We know that your idea is to own a vending machine, so go ahead and write that down now." Mikey wrote it down and showed it to Biz. "Good," said Biz. "Now let's see how much money it will take to get the business started. We can look on the computer to see how much vending machines cost."

Biz and Mikey got to work. After looking up prices on the computer, Biz said, "It looks like you will need $4000 to start: $3200 for the machines, $400 for snacks, and $400 for repairs." "Where am I going to get that type of money?" Mikey asked. Biz answered, "From sponsors, investors and loans. Sponsors are people who give you money that you don't have to pay back. Investors are people who give you money so they can own a piece of your business. A loan is money that you borrow. When a bank gives you a loan, you have to pay the money back. The funny thing is, you have to pay them back more than they gave you." Mikey smiled and took notes.

"Now, let's think about marketing," Biz said. "We need to know who your customers are and where you will place the machines so that your customers will see them and use them." "My customers will be kids, adults, and anyone who's looking for a snack," said Mikey. "I can put the machines at gyms, community centers, churches and office spaces." "Great!" said Biz. "Write that down." When Mikey finished writing, Biz said, "Now we have to get the word out about your business. Let's do some networking!" "Umm... What's networking again?" Mikey asked. Biz answered, "It's when you go out and meet people who can help you grow your business. Come on Mikey! Put on your best shirt and tie and let's go network!"

Mikey ran to his room and put on his black pants, white shirt and sports themed tie. They went to a networking event for business owners. Mikey learned a lot and met a lady who knew someone who wanted new vending machines for an office space! After the event, Mikey called the office and the owner invited him to move his machines in! Mikey and Biz were so excited! Then, they remembered that they still needed to raise the money to pay for the machines.

Mikey and Biz decided to ask Mikey's parents to be sponsors. Mikey was excited to show his parents his business plan. He told his parents that he had completed his business plan. "Mikey," his Mom said, "what do you know about a business plan?" Mikey explained what he learned while working on his business plan and told them about the office space that wanted him to move his machines in. Mikey's parents were amazed at all Mikey had done. His mom asked, "Mikey, how did you learn all this?" From this briefcase," said Mikey. "His name is Biz. He's my mentor." Mikey's parents were so excited, they didn't even realize that they were talking to a briefcase. "Mikey," they said," "we are so proud of you. You worked very hard, so we would like to support you by giving you a $2000 sponsorship." Mikey was excited. "Now I just need $2000 more!" he said.

Mikey decided to sell some lemonade to raise more money. He called his friend, Kendal, to ask him to help him with a lemonade stand. Mikey, Kendal and Biz made signs and flyers, then set up the lemonade stand. They sold a lot of lemonade, then went home to count their money. They made $980 dollars. Biz told the boys that, since they were business partners, they had to split the money they made. The boys got $490 apiece.

Mikey went back to his parents with his head down. "What's wrong champ?" said Mikey's dad. Mikey said, "I still don't have enough money." Just then, Mikey lifted up his head and said, "I know! I can ask family and friends to help!" Mikey and his mom started calling family and friends. Everyone was excited to help. After adding up all the money he got from family and friends, Mikey was still $20 short, so he decided to take out a small loan.

Now that Mikey had all the money he needed, it was time to pick out his vending machines! When Biz and Mikey got to the vending machine store, there were hundreds of machines to choose from. Mikey picked out a snack machine and a soda machine that he liked. When he was ready to order the machines and have them delivered to the office space, the store owner asked Mikey and Biz for the name of the business.

Mikey thought about it, then told Biz his idea for the name. "Let's call it 'Mikey's Munchies.' " Biz thought about it and said, " 'Mikey's Munchies.' Yeah, I like the sound of that." " 'Mikey's Munchies' it is!" the store owner said as he wrote the business name on the order form.

Biz was a great mentor to Mikey and Mikey put in a lot of hard work. Because of this, Mikey's Munchies became a huge success! Every week, Mikey would collect money from his vending machines. He just kept getting more and more money! He used his money to buy candy, video games, and all sorts of things! Mikey's business was so successful that other children wanted to learn from him. Soon, Mikey began teaching other children how to become business owners too! Everyone was so impressed and so proud of Mikey for what he had done. Mikey proved to everyone that with hard work and good mentorship, children can become great business owners.

## About the Author

Michael "Mikey" Wren is a 9 year old kid entrepreneur. He is the owner of Mikey's Munchies a vending machine business that he started when he was 8 years old. He's a member of Young Biz Kidz, a non-profit organization that encourage youth entrepreneurship. Mikey entrepreneurial journey was the inspiration for Mikey Learns about Business. Mikey's objective for his book is to help youth learn about business through his own experience.

22589069R00022

Made in the USA
San Bernardino, CA
14 January 2019